D1045154

A NOTE TO PARENTS

Reading Aloud with Your Child

Research shows that reading books aloud is the single most valuable support parents can provide in helping children learn to read.

- Be a ham! The more enthusiasm you display, the more your child will enjoy the book.
- Run your finger underneath the words as you read to signal that the print carries the story.
- Leave time for examining the illustrations more closely; encourage your child to find things in the pictures.
- Invite your youngster to join in whenever there's a repeated phrase in the text.
- Link up events in the book with similar events in your child's life.
- If your child asks a question, stop and answer it. The book can be a means to learning more about your child's thoughts.

Listening to Your Child Read Aloud

The support of your attention and praise is absolutely crucial to your child's continuing efforts to learn to read.

- If your child is learning to read and asks for a word, give it immediately so that the meaning of the story is not interrupted. DO NOT ask your child to sound out the word.
- On the other hand, if your child initiates the act of sounding out, don't intervene.
- If your child is reading along and makes what is called a miscue, listen for the sense of the miscue. If the word "road" is substituted for the word "street," for instance, no meaning is lost. Don't stop the reading for a correction.
- If the miscue makes no sense (for example, "horse" for "house"), ask your child to reread the sentence because you're not sure you understand what's just been read.
- Above all else, enjoy your child's growing command of print and make sure you give lots of praise. *You are your child's first teacher — and the most important one. Praise from you is critical for further risk-taking and learning.*

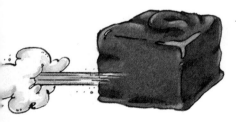

—Priscilla Lynch
Ph.D., New York University
Educational Consultant

To the voices on the other end of
computer help lines everywhere
— E.L.

For my sister, Karen
— D.B.

Text copyright © 1996 by Elizabeth Levy.
Illustrations copyright © 1996 by Denise Brunkus.
All rights reserved. Published by Scholastic Inc.
HELLO READER!, CARTWHEEL BOOKS, and the CARTWHEEL BOOKS logo
are registered trademarks of Scholastic Inc.

Library of Congress Cataloging-in-Publication Data
Levy, Elizabeth.
The creepy computer mystery / Elizabeth Levy ; illustrated by Denise
Brunkus.
   p.   cm. — (Hello reader! Level 4) (Invisible Inc. ; #4)
   Summary: When the Invisible Inc. gang makes computer greeting cards to
raise money to invite an author to school, they solve the mystery of the
author's real name.
   ISBN 0-590-60322-1
   [1. Computers — Fiction.   2. Schools — Fiction.   3. Moneymaking
projects — Fiction.   4. Mystery and detective stories.]
I. Brunkus, Denise, ill.   II. Title.   III. Series.   IV. Series: Levy, Elizabeth.
Invisible Inc. ; #4.
PZ7.L5827Cr   1996
[Fic]—dc20   95-30914
                                                                      CIP
                                                                      AC

12 11 10 9 8 7 6 5 4 3 2 1   6 7 8 9/9 0 1/0

                        Printed in the U.S.A.   24

            First Scholastic printing, February 1996

The
Creepy Computer Mystery

by Elizabeth Levy

Illustrated by
Denise Brunkus

Hello Reader! — Level 4

SCHOLASTIC INC. **Cartwheel** ·B·O·O·K·S·®

New York Toronto London Auckland Sydney

Chip fell into a strange pool of water. Now Chip is invisible. Justin knows how to read lips because of his hearing loss. Charlene is sometimes bossy, but always brave. Together they are Invisible Inc.— and they solve mysteries!

CHAPTER 1
Invitation to Doom

Justin sat at the computer. He tapped in his screen name, GonzoJust. The librarian, Ms. Grace, let him log in for the whole class. Today the class was going to go on-line with its favorite author, U.B. Spooks.

Justin loved to use the computer. Talking on the phone was hard for him because he couldn't hear well and he couldn't read lips over the phone. But on the computer, Justin didn't have to hear. He could read instead.

"Get your questions ready!" said Charlene.

"I want to ask about *Slime on the Playground*," said Chip. "That was awesome."

"You're invisible slime," Keith said to Chip. "I bet U.B. Spooks could write a book about you."

Chip gave Keith an angry look, but Keith didn't know. That was one of the problems with being invisible. Nobody could see your face when you were mad or sad.

"It's time. It's time!" shouted Justin.

The screen showed the cover of U.B. Spooks' newest book, *Poison in the Lunch Room*.

On-line Host: Good afternoon. We know you are eager to meet U.B. Spooks. But, please remember, U.B. Spooks might not be able to answer all questions.

U.B. Spooks: Hi, everybody out there!

Justin quickly typed in the first question. *Will you come to our school? We have an invisible boy here.*

But the words didn't appear on the monitor.

Justin frowned. Questions were getting through from other classes around the country. But not from theirs.

Question: If you weren't an author what would you be?

U.B. Spooks: That's a funny question. Because I'm not only an author. I have another job, but I like to keep it private.

Question: Where do you get your ideas?

U.B. Spooks: From everywhere. From everything I see and hear and from people all around me. I'm always looking for new ideas.

Question: What do the initials U.B. stand for?

U.B. Spooks: U.B. Spooks is my pen name. I guess I just like the sound of "ooo."

Question: Why do you use a pen name?

U.B. Spooks: I like to keep the two sides of my life separate. Nobody I

work with knows that I am an author.

"What do you think the other job is?" asked Keith.

"Why aren't our questions getting in there?" asked Charlene.

"Give me time," said Justin. He banged on the keys. They were frozen.

"Whoops," said Justin. "Whoops" is not a word that anybody likes to hear around a computer.

"What's wrong?" asked Ms. Grace. Ms. Grace hated when anything went wrong with the library's computer.

"The keys are frozen," said Justin.

"But it's warm in here," said Charlene.

"Not really frozen. It just means that I can't type anything," said Justin.

"Maybe too many people are trying to get through," said Sandy.

"Won't we get to ask our questions?" asked Mary. "Maybe we should raise our hands."

Charlene put her hands on her hips. "Don't be silly, Mary. The author is on a computer somewhere. U.B. Spooks can't see us raise our hands!"

"I was making a joke," said Mary.

"The keys are okay now!" said Justin. He repeated his question.

Question: Would you like to come to a school where you'd meet an invisible boy?

Suddenly the screen went blank!

"Whoops!" Justin said again.

"I wish you would stop saying that!" said Charlene.

"What's wrong?" asked Ms. Grace.

"I don't know," said Justin. He

tapped the escape button, but nothing worked. Meanwhile, Chip was sulking in the corner. That was another problem with being invisible. Nobody noticed when you were sulking.

"You've got to get us back on-line," said Charlene.

"Give me a second! Give me a second!" mumbled Justin. He hated messing up on the computer. It gave him a stomachache. Justin kept attacking the escape key.

"Hey, look!" shouted Charlene. She pointed to the screen.

"What's that?" asked Charlene.

Then the symbols changed into letters that read:

INVITATION TO DOOM!

CHAPTER 2
Great Minds
Think Alike

Suddenly the screen went blank again and the modem made funny noises.

"What's happening?" asked Ms. Grace.

"We're cut off," said Justin.

Charlene shivered. "We're invited to doom."

"Doom," mumbled Chip. "I don't like the sound of that."

"What's the matter, invisible boy? Is it a little too scary for you?" said Keith.

"Keith, that's not the way you talk to someone in my library... or anywhere for that matter," said Ms. Grace.

Chip stuck out his tongue at Keith. Chip would get in trouble for doing that if the librarian saw him. But, of course, Ms. Grace couldn't see his tongue. That was the good news about being invisible. The teachers never saw when you stuck out your tongue. The bad news was that neither could Keith. Chip rolled his eyes up toward the ceiling. Sometimes being invisible was really tough!

"What are we going to do about this invitation to doom?" Charlene asked.

"Nothing," said Chip. "What can we do about it?"

"But we have to find out who sent this," said Charlene. "We're Invisible Inc. and we solve mysteries. It's our job!"

"Well, we know one thing," said Justin. "The person who sent that message knows how to use a computer."

The next day Ms. Grace printed out the live chat with U.B. Spooks. She gave it to Justin.

Justin read through the chat. "I can't believe it. Here was our chance to invite U.B. Spooks to our school. But none of our questions went through. U.B. Spooks doesn't even know we exist."

"We could ask him to our school through regular mail," said Ms. Grace. "I'll write to his publisher. But we'll have to raise the money to pay for his expenses and a fee."

"We can do that," said Charlene.

Justin felt cheerful again. Maybe U.B. Spooks could come to their school after all. Justin got busy at the computer. He was making a birthday card for his mom. He made a picture of a birthday cake. Then he used the mouse to color the cake purple, his mother's favorite color.

"That's beautiful," said Ms. Grace.

"Wait a minute! Wait a minute! Incoming idea!" shouted Charlene. Charlene always got excited about her own ideas. She jumped up and down.

"I've got one, too!" said Sandy. "We could raise money to get U.B. Spooks by selling computer greeting cards."

Charlene stared at her. "That was my idea!"

"Well, you know what we say on the computer. . . GMTA!" Justin typed the letters GMTA into the computer.

"What does that mean?" asked Chip. It was the first thing he had said in a long time.

"Great Minds Think Alike!" said Justin. He looked at Chip, who was working at the computer next to him. "Come on, buddy. You've got a computer. You know what the shorthand means."

"Yeah," said Chip. Chip did have a computer at home, but he wasn't as good on it as Justin.

"Making cards is an excellent idea," said Ms. Grace. "The PTA will buy cards. They always need invitations."

"We can make posters to advertise," said Sandy.

Justin sat at the computer while the other kids made suggestions.

"Let's make the letters bigger!"

"Let's make the letters fatter!"

"Let's make the words look like a heart."

"Pink and purple letters!"

"No! Red and blue letters!"

Justin was working so hard that he never noticed that Chip had walked away.

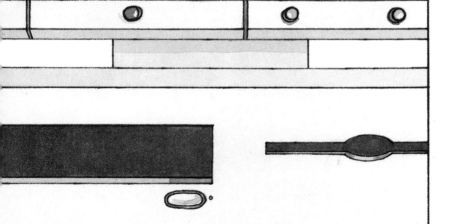

Justin finished the ad and sent it to the printer. But the library printer was backed up with other print jobs. And it was time for the class to go back to its room.

After recess the boys and girls went back to the library to get the copies of their poster. But instead of their posters, two pieces of paper were waiting for them. One read . . .

: — (: — B

The other paper read:

> ## "BEWARE! Especially you, the girl who likes to boss people around — and you — the boy who is so good with computers. You and your friend, the bossy girl, are invited to . . . DOOM!"

"Hey," said Sandy. "Do you think the boy who's so good with computers could be Justin?"

"Wait a minute! Wait a minute!" Charlene wondered out loud. "Who's the bossy girl?"

Everybody stared at Charlene.

"The computer is writing about us!" said Justin.

He turned the first piece of paper around. "It's computer shorthand. Look at it sideways. **: - (** is a frowning face.

"I'm not exactly sure what **: - B** means, but **: - P** means 'I'm sticking my tongue out at you.' Someone is mad at us."

Nobody could see that the corners of Chip's mouth were turned down.

CHAPTER 3
Run-Away Candy

The orders for greeting cards came in fast. The PTA ordered invitations to the Book Fair. The new school secretary, Mrs. Skoops, bought thank-you cards.

"Maybe you could add 'Thank you for writing,'" she said.

"Thank you for writing what?" asked Charlene.

"Oh, uh . . . I get lots of mail," said Mrs. Skoops.

One of the kindergartners wanted invitations for her birthday party.

"I'm going to have the Puffy Players at my party," said Roshanna. "Can you draw pictures of them on the card?"

"Sure," said Charlene. "What do they look like?"

Roshanna shrugged. "I don't know."

Charlene's little brother, Stanley, turned to Roshanna. "I think you should get your cards at a store."

"Hey," said Charlene. "We're doing this for something important. We're going to ask U.B. Spooks to come to our school."

"Our teacher says that the kindergartners won't be invited," said Stanley. "The books are too scary. It's not fair."

"Life's not fair," Charlene said to her brother.

"Don't worry, Roshanna," Justin said. "We'll make great invitations. We'll go see what the Puffy Players look like!"

"We will?" said Charlene. "But we don't have time. We have a mystery to solve."

"It's more important to raise money to get U.B. Spooks!" Justin said.

After school, Chip got on his bicycle to go home. "Hey, Chip!" shouted Justin. "Aren't you coming with us?"

"No. I have to go home to walk Max," said Chip.

There was something odd in Chip's voice.

"We'll go with you," said Charlene. "We can pick up Max and then go to see the Puffy Players. Then we can try to find out who is trying to scare Invisible Inc."

She and Justin walked with Chip over to his house.

"You've been very quiet lately," said Charlene.

"You all have been so busy trying to get that author to come," said Chip.

"What do you mean, *you* all? Don't you mean, *we*?" asked Charlene. "We're Invisible Inc. We stick together."

"But I'm the only one who's invisible," Chip said to himself.

When they got to Chip's house, Max was glad to see them. The little brown tip of his tail waved back and forth. While Chip went upstairs, Justin looked at the papers around Chip's computer.

"What's taking Chip so long?" Charlene asked.

"Nothing," said Chip. "I've been down here for five minutes!"

Chip had changed into his invisible clothes.

"Well, let's get going," said Charlene. "We've got to go meet the Puffy Players." Justin put down the papers.

The Puffy Players had offices right above the little stationery store at the mall. Charlene, Justin, Chip, and Max walked up the stairs. They heard voices singing "Old MacDonald Had a Farm."

Max barked every time he heard an "oink, oink."

Justin knocked on the door. "Who's there?"

"Justin McCabe!" shouted Justin.

"Just in time!" said a voice behind the door. Justin rolled his eyes. He had heard that knock-knock joke before.

The door was opened by a man in a big puffy pig outfit. A woman was in a cat outfit. Max growled at the cat.

"Who's growling?" asked the pig.

"Quiet, Max," said Chip.

"Who said that?" asked a bunny.

"Me," said Chip.

The bunny stared into space. "Is one of you kids throwing your voice?"

"No," said Chip. "I'm invisible."

"Oh, we've heard about an invisible kid in town," said the pig.

Chip held on tight to Max's leash. He didn't really like being known as "that invisible kid."

"We're making invitations for a birthday party for a girl who hired you. Our customer wanted us to draw a picture of you," Charlene said.

"Sounds good," said the pig. "We usually get our ads printed downstairs at the stationery store. But show us what you come up with. Maybe we'll use you."

Charlene and Justin were smiling as they left the shop. "That's great. Isn't it, Chip?" said Charlene. She looked around. Chip had disappeared. "Chip?"

"Charlene," said Justin. "Something's wrong with Chip. I know it."

Justin saw Chip's knapsack by the curb. It was dented. Then he saw Max's leash. Justin poked above the knapsack.

"Chip?" asked Justin. "Are you sitting on your knapsack?"

"Go away," said Chip.

"What's wrong?" asked Justin.

Before Chip could answer, Charlene broke in. "What do they sell at a stationery store?" she asked.

"Stationery," said Chip. "Is this another dumb knock-knock joke . . . like the one the pig asked?"

"I thought the pig was cute," said Charlene. "But no. It's not a joke. I bet the store is losing money because people are starting to come to us for their cards. What if the stationery store owner is sending us scary notes so we'll quit?"

Justin scowled. "The scary messages started before we began making cards," he said.

"Maybe the first one was just a kid fooling around . . . and then the stationery store owner heard about our card business and sent the next scary message," said Charlene.

"Hmmm," said Justin. "It's true. Lots of people from the school go in there. Look, there goes Mrs. Skoops."

"I'm sure I've solved the crime," said Charlene. "We'll go into the stationery store and pretend to buy something. You stay invisible and sneak into the owner's office. Find out if his computer is hooked up to the one in the school library."

"You really are bossy sometimes," said Chip.

Chip hopped up. He gave Charlene his knapsack and snuck into the stationery store with Max.

Inside the store, Mrs. Skoops was buying paper. The store owner turned to Charlene and Justin. "May I help you kids?" he asked.

Mrs. Skoops screamed. She pointed toward the floor. A piece of candy was floating in the air.

Charlene whispered to Justin, "Max must have slipped out of his collar. We're in big trouble now!"

Suddenly the candy hopped up to the counter. The owner's eyes opened wide. "What was that?" he said.

"We'd better leave," said Charlene quickly. She and Justin ran out of the store. They met Chip and Max outside.

"That was close," said Chip. "Anyhow, I went into the owner's office. He didn't even have a computer."

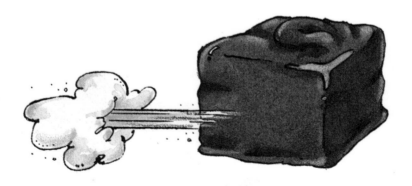

Charlene sighed. "I guess we have to forget about him as a suspect. We're back at the beginning. I think we have to look closer at everybody at school."

"Maybe even closer than that," said Justin thoughtfully.

CHAPTER 4
Not a Freak—a Friend!

Chip sat down at his usual place during computer time. He was surprised to find a message for him:

Chip. I know your secret.
But **: - X**.

The message was signed GonzoJust. Chip rubbed his eyes. He tried very hard to remember how to read the symbol.

: - X was a face with its lips closed. It was the sign for keeping a secret. Justin was saying that he wouldn't tattle.

At recess, Chip met Justin near their favorite tree.

"How did you know it was me?" Chip asked into Justin's good ear.

"You've been acting funny all week," said Justin. "When I was at your house, I was looking at the papers around your computer. There was a mistake. On your paper it said **: - B** for sticking out your tongue instead of **: - P**—just like on the paper I found at school. Why did you want to stick out your tongue?"

"You told the author to come to

school to meet the invisible kid," said Chip. "It made me feel like a freak... not a friend. No one can ever see how I feel, so I used the computer to show it."

Justin put his hand on Chip's shoulder. "I'm sorry," he said. "I guess I didn't think. I got used to your being invisible. I didn't think you minded."

"Don't you mind sometimes that you have to wear a phonic ear and that you have trouble hearing?" Chip asked.

"Yeah," said Justin.

"Well, it's not always fun to be invisible either," said Chip. He patted Justin on the shoulder. All of a sudden they saw Charlene running toward them.

"Justin! Chip! Come quick!"

shouted Charlene. "I just went into
the library to pick up the invitations
we made for Roshanna's birthday
party. They're ruined! Look at this."
Charlene showed them the cards.

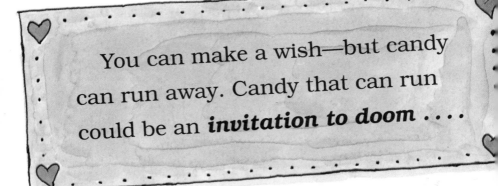

You can make a wish—but candy
can run away. Candy that can run
could be an *invitation to doom* . . . .

"That stuff about invitation to
doom doesn't belong on a birthday
invitation for little kids!" Charlene
said. "We've got to catch the person

who's been sending these terrible messages!"

"We have caught the person," said Justin. "Chip, I think you'd better tell her."

"Tell her what?" said Chip. "I didn't do anything to Roshanna's invitations."

"What about the PTA Book Fair announcements? And all the other *invitations to doom* that came out of the printer?" asked Justin.

"That wasn't me! I just sent the one note . . . sticking my tongue out at everybody. I was mad because

nobody can ever really see me frown or stick out my tongue."

"Didn't you write all that invitation to doom stuff?" asked Justin.

"Of course not. Who do you think I am, U.B. Spooks?" asked Chip.

CHAPTER 5
Too Weird to Be True

Chip took one of Roshanna's birthday invitations and read it again. "'Candy that can run by itself.' It sounds like Max in the stationery store."

"It does!" said Charlene. "But if you didn't write it, who did?"

"Spooks!" said Justin.

"Where?" said Charlene. "Who are you trying to scare?"

"Spooks! Right here! Right in our school!" said Justin mysteriously. "Let's go to the library."

"U.B. Spooks likes the sound of 'ooo,'" said Justin. "Who else do we know who has a name with 'ooo' in it?"

"Mrs. Skoops?" asked Charlene. "But she's so nice."

"Nice and spooky," said Justin. "SKOOPS spelled backward is SPOOKS!"

Justin asked Ms. Grace if he could have a copy of U.B. Spooks' *Slime on the Playground*. "I'm going to get it autographed."

Ms. Grace looked very confused.

Justin, Chip, and Charlene took the book to the office. Mrs. Skoops looked up from her work. "Hi, kids," she said. "What can I do for you?"

"Can you autograph this book for me?" said Justin.

Mrs. Skoops put her hand over her mouth. She looked embarrassed. "How did you know?"

"We're Invisible Inc. We know everything," bragged Charlene. "We even know you're next book is *Invitation to Doom!* And we know that one of your characters is like me and one of your characters is like Justin."

"How did you know that?" Mrs. Skoops asked.

"We keep getting your printouts in the library," said Chip.

"I wondered what happened to them," said Mrs. Skoops. "If I don't connect my computer the right way in the morning, my copies go all over the place! I've been searching high and low for the new chapter that I've been writing during my break."

"Well, it went to the library," said Justin. "And it kept getting into our invitations. We were raising money to bring you to the school and you're already here."

"I know," said Mrs. Skoops. "But I couldn't tell you until I finished my new book. I like my characters to seem real. So I study real kids to find out what they do. That's why I took this job."

"Real kids solve mysteries," said Chip.

"And you're very good at it," said Mrs. Skoops.

"Are you going to put an invisible boy in your next story?" asked Charlene.

Mrs. Skoops smiled. "I don't know," she said. "It's almost too unusual to be true. Would anyone believe it?"

"We would," said Charlene and
Justin together. They put their arms
around Chip.